GIANNA

Mamie Jean Calvert

First edition December 2020

ISBN: 978-1-7361994-0-4

The information contained in this book is intended to be for entertainment purposes only.

Edited by Judy Nessen
Cover Photography by Gianna Rivelli
Design Layout by Stephen Morgan

Learn more at
www.imdb.com / Mamie Jean Calvert

DEDICATION

In honor of my beautiful daughter, Angela Kay Rivelli, who left us for Heaven on April 23, 2015. We can imagine her doing all the things she loves — singing, dancing, cooking, watching the butterflies in her garden, playing with her dogs, and smiling at everyone she meets. You are thought of today and every day because we all love and miss you so much.

CONTENTS

FOREWORD

Mamie Jean Calvert is a whirlwind of ideas and imagination. I have known her for many years, and she continues to amaze me with her ability to whip out a story in a short period of time. As a writer, producer, director, actor, mentor … she is constantly creative. As an editor/proofreader, I have had the privilege of working with her on numerous projects over the years. Her Southern roots are reflected in her writing. I have tried to keep the essence of Mamie and her way of communicating. I hope I have succeeded. How would I describe Mamie in one word? I don't think that's possible. There isn't one word that would be adequate. Enjoy the book; I know I did.

~*Judy Nessen*

PREFACE

Gianna is an Italian name with two meanings: "God is gracious" or "The Lord is gracious."

This is a story of life in the deep South. Helen (Granny) Wallace faces many trials and tribulations, but through the little country church that means so much to her she never loses her faith. Johnny, her only son, also faces hardships that turn his life upside down for many years. Their worlds change when a little girl comes into their lives.

This book is inspired by a script I wrote and decided to turn into a book because I love the story. Being born and raised in Irvine, Kentucky, a lot of the story holds true. I didn't grow up poor, but I sure could relate to a lot of folks who were. This is just a story of life with a happy ending; I hope everyone has a happy ending as well.

I hope you enjoy reading this book as much as I enjoyed writing it.

Mamie Jean

Chapter 1

The Marriage

*H*elen Wallace sits on her wrap-around porch, gently swaying back and forth in her rocking chair. Her long dark hair flows in the wind. Her blue eyes sparkle as she glances toward the sky and then stares into her garden. She is proud of the green beans and tomatoes she has grown to help with the grocery bill. But her thoughts change as she rubs her pregnant belly. How could Matt leave her at a time like this? Matt had been her high school sweetheart. A quarterback, so good looking, with his deep green eyes and blonde hair – he could have anyone, but he picked her. Matt was wonderful until they got married. They had a small wedding with a few friends. She wore a short white dress and carried a bouquet of white and red roses. Matt stood over six feet tall. His slender build made him look so handsome in his dark blue pin-striped suit.

Three months into the marriage, she found out she was pregnant. Matt was furious. "No one can get pregnant that soon. I mean, we messed around for years!"

Helen didn't know what to say to that. "It was just right, now."

Matt's reply? "You have been messing around with someone else."

She was crushed. How could he accuse her of being with someone else? He should know better, with her being of Christian faith, she very much tried to live by the Bible. Helen screamed at him. "You know that is not true, you are the only one I have been with." Matt left her anyway.

Helen was now on her own and pregnant. *At least*, she thought, *I have a job as a waitress at the Pine Café*. She had been working there for years. Everyone liked her; she was so pretty, and she had a great personality. She was also a hard worker. It was hard not to like her. She made enough money to get by, but knew now with a child coming things would be different.

Helen lived at the edge of town in a tiny white house, trimmed in light blue. She walked to work every day. It was a small town called Lower Bend, Kentucky. It was easy to get around without a car, since she didn't have one. It's what you call in Kentucky poor, or poor white trash.

Chapter 2

Pregnant and Scared

*H*elen, now at the end of her pregnancy, goes into labor. Her labor pains are two minutes apart. She paces the floor. She has everything laid out: the pan for water, the white towels, and all the things the midwife she met at the grocery store told her to have ready. She double checks the cash in the envelope, three hundred dollars; the midwife had asked for cash. Helen holds her belly; the pains are one minute apart. Now breathing hard, she hopes that the midwife will be knocking on the door any minute now.

The pain is getting severe; she runs and unlocks the front door and lies down on the bed. After being in pain for a few more minutes, she hears the knock on the front door. Helen yells, "Come in, the door is open." The door swings open and a big woman appears. She is dressed in white, looking more like a man than a woman. "Please hurry," Helen screams. "The baby is coming!" Helen didn't remember the midwife being so big and scary, but she is in too much pain to worry about that now.

3

Helen has a difficult birth. The midwife pulls and tugs on the baby boy. By the time the birth is over, the midwife has crippled the baby. Helen knows that something is wrong, but she is just glad he has all his fingers and toes. She is happy to give the midwife the money and get her out of her house.

Helen names him Johnny, after her father. His little leg turns the wrong way. Helen blames herself for not checking out the midwife, who she finds out later is not certified. She feels guilty for her son being crippled. She tries to do everything to make it up to him. She saves money, goes without food for herself to take him to the best doctors she can find in the area. They all say the same – "Nothing we can do for him, the way his leg had been pulled. Just pray." Pray she did, all the time. They attended church every Sunday, and she hoped for a miracle.

Chapter 3

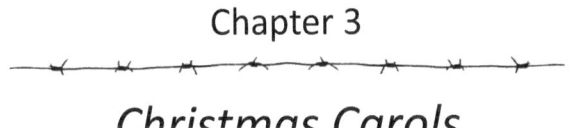

Christmas Carols

*J*ohnny is a great kid and never blames anyone for his disability, especially his mom. All he wants to do is grow up, get a good job, and take care of her. He hates that she has to work all the time. He loves her so much, and not once does he ever ask to see his dad.

The years go by. Johnny is now twelve, and they are poorer than ever. There is not as much business at the café, since the only big factory in town has closed. Johnny keeps his head up. He does extremely well in school because he has nothing else to keep him busy.

One of his favorite things to do is to walk down the dirt lane with his homemade walking stick to the little white Southern Baptist church, the one that his mother and father got married in. He loves listening to the kids sing Christmas carols.

The church is rehearsing for a Christmas pageant. They practice every Thursday, and that is where Johnny goes. He is dressed in ragged clothes and never once thinks of entering the church. None of the children pay any attention to him; they enter into the church one by one, laughing and talking. Johnny just sits down on the church steps, listens to the music, and whittles on a piece of wood. He is making a Christmas present for his mom. She loves lions, and he is determined to make her one.

While Johnny is sitting on the church steps whittling, his best and only friend, Mike Nessen, comes down the lane toward the church. He is wearing faded jeans and a coat too big for him. He sits down by Johnny. He is also twelve but is nothing like Johnny; Mike has a chip on his shoulder and is never in a good mood.

Johnny is curious. "How did you know I was here?"

"Your mama said you sometimes walk here on one of your good days ... this one of your good days?"

"I'm fine."

"Fine?"

"Mike, I don't want to talk about it."

"Okay by me."

Johnny keeps his head down and continues whittling.

"Whatcha makin'?"

"Something for my mama. It's Christmas, you know?"

Mike runs his fingers through his long dark hair, then says with his rough voice, "Yes. Don't remind me.

Don't you wish you could just go out and buy your mama a Christmas present?"

"Oh, I don't know. I like to make her presents. It's the thought that counts."

"Yeah, if you say so. I am only sure of one thing, Johnny."

Johnny stops whittling and looks up at Mike. "What's that, Mike?"

"Mike Nessen ain't gonna be pissant poor all his life." Johnny stares at Mike and doesn't say anything. "Christmas at my house is just another reason to buy a bigger jug of wine."

Johnny realizes that he and his mom might not have much, but no one drinks and he knows how much his mom loves him. "I am sorry, Mike."

"Don't be, I'm used to it." Mike quickly changes the subject. "You really like this Christmas music, Johnny?"

"I love it."

Mike gets up to leave and then turns and looks at Johnny. "Did you want me to walk you home, Johnny?"

"No thanks. I'm fine, but come over to our house if you like."

"Thanks. I'll be okay."

Mike turns and starts walking down the lane; he stops and looks back at Johnny, who is watching him. Johnny feels bad for Mike, whose family doesn't care much about him. Both his parents are alcoholics. Johnny thinks how that big ragged coat makes Mike look much older than his tiny self. Johnny hollers, "Merry Christmas, Mike!"

Mike stops for a long moment and looks at Johnny. He shrugs his shoulders. "Merry Christmas … Johnny."

Chapter 4

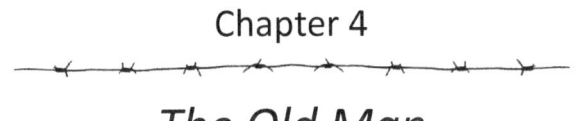

The Old Man

*E*veryone leaves the church and no one pays any attention to Johnny; it is like he isn't even there. Johnny has fallen asleep on the church steps. Beside him are his knife and the piece of wood he was whittling on. He wakes up; it takes him a few moments to realize where he is. He raises his head and looks around. He is all alone. Johnny picks up the knife and the wooden lion, ready to go home. He stands up and begins descending the steps when all of a sudden a sharp pain hits him hard, doubling him over. He drops the knife and lion and falls face down into the dirt. He has passed out for a few moments. Then he raises his head and rubs the dirt off the lion on his pants. He looks up, shocked at what he sees. An old man stands in front of him, dressed in a tattered, long dark robe; a hood covers his head. Johnny can't see all of the old man's face. The only thing he can see is his eyes, and they look so kind.

The old man reaches down and helps Johnny get up. The man picks up the knife, wipes the dirt off on his robe, then hands it back to Johnny. He then reaches into his pocket, takes out a ring, and puts it on Johnny's finger. The ring immediately glows a strange green light. Johnny is half scared, half surprised. He stares at the ring on his finger. The old man starts to talk; it's the softest voice Johnny has ever heard: "Merry Christmas, Johnny. Wear this ring, and good health and luck will always be with you."

The old man picks up the homemade walking stick and breaks it in two, throws it to the ground, turns and walks down the dirt lane, never looking back. Johnny watches the old man until he disappears, seemingly vanishing into thin air. Still in shock, Johnny runs his hand through his dirty blonde hair. He gets up and to his surprise he can walk, and walk without a cane.

Chapter 5

Johnny All Grown Up

Johnny marries a wonderful girl named Priscilla. She moved into his home town when he was a senior in high school. She is a thin, beautiful woman with long, curly dark hair, and full of life. The moment he saw Priscilla, he fell in love with her. His mother Helen was so happy for him. He dated Priscilla all through college and then he proposed to her at their graduation. They got married in the spring at the same white Southern Baptist church where Johnny used to sit on the steps listening to Christmas carols and was healed by the mysterious old man.

Johnny and Priscilla now live in a white, two-story home. A picket fence surrounds the house. Trees fill the yard like a forest. He has been working outside all day and is looking forward to surprising Priscilla with all the Christmas decorations he has put up. Christmas is her favorite time of the year. He wants it to be beautiful for her. He finishes all the decorations and stands back to admire his work.

A facsimile of Santa and his reindeer are on the

roof of the house. A large Christmas tree can be seen in the front picture window. Johnny turns on all the lights as Priscilla opens the door and sticks her head out. "Can I come and look now?"

"Yes, come on out."

Priscilla exits slowly from the house. She is beautiful; she has a certain glow about her. She is now in her mid-twenties; her hair is tied back in a pony tail. She weighs a little more now since she is eight months pregnant. She is wearing a powder blue maternity dress. She walks slowly as not to fall, carrying a tray of homemade chocolate chip cookies, Johnny's favorite.

Priscilla admires the house. "Oh Johnny, it's beautiful. Thank you so much, I love it."

They look up into the sky and say together, "Thank you for our blessings and our child who is about to come into this world. Amen."

Johnny takes a few cookies from the tray. "I love them and I love you." He leans down and gives Priscilla a big kiss. "These are my favorite cookies."

Priscilla, smiling, says, "I know, that is why I made so many."

Johnny and Priscilla stare at the decorated house and eat cookies. Light rain starts to fall. Thunder roars in the distance; lightning lights up the sky. They laugh and run into the house. Suddenly Priscilla has a sharp pain in her stomach.

Chapter 6

The Accident

*J*ohnny and Priscilla are in the car heading to the hospital. The rain is falling hard. Headlights coming toward them on the road make it hard for Johnny to see. The rain comes down harder. He grabs a rag from under the seat and tries to wipe off the inside of the window. The car speeds down the highway. The rain turns to snow and sleet, making the road like ice to drive on. The car slides around a curve. Johnny tries to see out the windshield and every few seconds wipes the fog off the windows. Priscilla is now doubled up in pain.

"Oh Johnny, hurry! I think the baby is coming!"

Johnny can hear the fear in her voice. "Just try and hold on."

The snow and sleet are coming down hard, and Johnny drives faster. Suddenly he sees headlights coming directly toward him in his lane. He swerves to avoid a head-on collision. The oncoming car sideswipes Johnny's car, causing it to go into a spin, sliding sideways across the road and into a tree.

Priscilla screams. The ring on Johnny's finger glows as it did when the old man gave it to him. Priscilla, still screaming, grabs his hand; in doing so, she pulls the ring off his finger. The other car's brake lights come on as it stops for a moment, then races off into the night.

Chapter 7

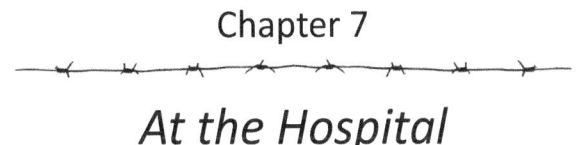

At the Hospital

*J*ohnny paces the floor of the waiting room. He has scratches and dried blood on his face. Helen comes running into the room. Now in her early fifties, her hair silver, she is wearing an old, drab coat. She hurries over to Johnny and touches his face. "Son, what happened?"

Pulling away from her, Johnny sobs. "I wrecked the car … the snow … the ice ... I don't know what happened."

Helen tries to reassure him. "I'm sure everything will be okay."

At that moment a doctor comes into the waiting room, a sad expression on his face. Johnny runs over and grabs him. "Please say she's all right!"

The doctor looks at Helen and Johnny. "I'm sorry, there was nothing we could do."

Helen cries, "Oh God, no!"

Johnny goes into a rage, crying and going crazy. "No! No! No! It just can't be! Why wasn't it me? She didn't deserve to die."

Johnny looks straight into the eyes of the doctor. "And the baby?"

The doctor shakes his head no. Johnny grabs the doctor and starts to beat on him. Helen runs over to them. "Johnny, please stop; it wasn't his fault."

"No, it was mine. I killed my wife and baby."

Two orderlies come running down the hall and pull Johnny off the doctor. Johnny stands in the middle of the room like a mad dog, screaming "I killed my wife and baby!" He pulls away and runs out the door, breaking the two front door windows on his way out.

Helen stares at the broken glass, watching Johnny disappear into the darkness of the night. She walks over to the doctor and quietly asks, "I am so sorry. Are you all right?"

The doctor replies, "It's okay, I understand his pain."

Helen tries again to apologize to the doctor.

"Not to worry, he is out of his mind right now."

Helen looks at the doctor. "Can I go in and see her?" The doctor shakes his head yes.

Johnny, in the hospital parking lot, goes from car to car to see if one might be unlocked. He sees a Harley and gets on it, starts it, and roars off into the night.

In the hospital, Helen enters the all-white room. Priscilla is still hooked up to the numerous machines. The one that monitors her heart shows a flat line.

Helen slowly walks over to her. With tears in her eyes, she leans down and kisses Priscilla on the cheek. "I love you, honey, rest in peace."

All of a sudden Helen thinks she sees Priscilla's stomach move. She looks, and then she looks again. The stomach is moving and the resumption of heart activity starts to beep on the monitor. Helen sees a green light coming out of Priscilla's clenched hand. She opens the hand and in it is Johnny's ring, glowing brighter than ever. The resumption of the heart activity gets stronger. Helen screams. "Oh my God! Doctor, doctor! Please come in here!"

Chapter 8

Johnny Goes Crazy

*T*he bike Johnny stole from the hospital parking lot is up against a tree and he is lying on the ground. A whiskey bottle and beer cans litter the area around him. A semi rolls by on the lonely highway; the sound of the brakes wakes him up. Johnny stumbles up from the ground. He goes over to a tree to take a leak. He looks like a bum. Getting back on the stolen Harley, he hits the road. Johnny tries to take a drink from his liquor bottle but it's empty; he tosses the bottle into a ditch. He looks up and sees a sign that indicates he is coming into Los Angeles. He plans to head to the first liquor store he sees.

Johnny is unaware that the liquor store is being watched by two undercover cops sitting in the front seat of an unmarked police car. One of the cops, Mike, impatiently drums his fingers on the steering wheel. "God, I hate this."

The other cop, Harold, looks at Mike. "What?"

"Stakeout. Undercover. Whatever the hell you want to call it. It's boring. I miss the action of a black and white patrol."

"So transfer back. But give me the names of your sources before you do."

Mike gives Harold a dirty look. "You know I will never reveal my sources."

Johnny sees the liquor store up ahead in the distance. He sees two bikers, rough looking, on Harleys pull up in front of the store and cut their engines.

Back in the undercover car, Mike says, "Looks like the Harley Gang is right on time."

Harold replies, "I thought there were three of them on the last job they pulled."

At that moment, Johnny pulls up by the bikers and cuts his engine. Mike exclaims, "Bingo! Call in for backup. I don't want to get my hands dirty."

Chapter 9

Trouble at the Liquor Store

Johnny is dirty, unshaven, and a little drunk. He parks his bike and walks over to the two bikers, George and Lopez, who have just parked their bikes and are getting off as Johnny walks up to them. They give him a mean look; they are not pleased to see him. Johnny leans over and gets into the face of one of the bikers. "You got a match?"

The biker, George, growls, "What do you want a match for, punk?"

Johnny, unintimidated, says, "For the cigarette I'm gonna borrow."

Lopez starts to laugh. George says, "For a little guy, you sure got guts." Lopez hands Johnny a cigarette and lights it for him. George, winking at his buddy Lopez, says, "We're gonna buy some beer and party. Wanna party, kid?" Johnny pulls a half pint of whiskey out of his pocket. Seeing that it's empty, he throws it on the pavement, where it shatters.

Johnny enters the liquor store first; George and Lopez are right behind him. Johnny goes over to the cooler and pulls out a six-pack of beer. George is at the counter with a gun pulled on the cashier. "Raise 'em!" Johnny realizes what is happening. He drops the beer to the floor and runs to the front door. George laughs and fires a shot at Johnny as he flies out the door and falls onto the pavement.

At that moment two black-and-white police cars screech into the parking lot. The unmarked police car also races in and stops; Mike and Harold jump out of the car. Harold, wearing sunglasses even though it's night because he thinks it makes him look cool, grabs Johnny. Johnny hears shots ring out in the background. Harold throws Johnny up against the car. Johnny's wallet falls to the ground. Harold cuffs Johnny and shoves him into the back seat of the car. Johnny starts to say something and tries to get out. Harold yells, "Shut up and be quiet. We'll deal with you later."

Johnny, looking at Harold, says, "I didn't do anything."

Harold snarls. "That's what they all say."

Johnny tries again to get out of the car, but Harold pushes him back in and punches him in the stomach. Johnny decides to be quiet. Then he sees the other officer walk over and pick up the dropped wallet. Johnny notices he is wearing a gold I.D. bracelet with the initials M.N. The officer flips through the wallet. He looks a little surprised when he sees that it belongs to Johnny Wallace. He flips it shut and says to Harold, "Let him go."

"What?"

"I said let him go."

Harold pulls Johnny out of the car, takes off the cuffs, shoves him to the ground, and growls, "Now get out of here."

Johnny wastes no time running to his bike. He can still hear shots being fired in the background. A stray bullet hits him, grazing his head. He falls to the ground.

George and Lopez, with their hands behind their backs, are led out of the store by the policemen. George gives Johnny a kick in the head as he walks by. Johnny groans. Lopez spits on Johnny as he walks by. Mike knocks Lopez to the ground.

George hollers to the policemen as they lead him to the patrol car. "A cop lover, I guess?"

Mike looks at George and Lopez. "Get them out of here."

Chapter 10

In a Strange Motel

*J*ohnny is lying in bed; there's a white bandage on his forehead. He stirs and wakes up, looking around at a strange room, and not remembering how he got there. He gets out of bed, clad only in his white shorts. He grimaces and touches his head, feeling the bandage. Then he walks to the bathroom and looks in the mirror. Seeing a large scrape across his head, he remembers the bikers he ran into at the liquor store. Walking over to the window and looking out, Johnny sees the Harley sitting in the parking lot of a rundown motel.

He walks back toward the bed and gets dressed. He sees his wallet laying on the nightstand and picks it up. As he opens the wallet a business card falls out. He picks it up and reads out loud: "Los Angeles Police Department, Mike Nessen." Johnny rubs his thumb across the replica of the police badge on the card. A look of disbelief crosses his face. He thinks to himself, *"That is why he let me go."* He puts the card back inside his wallet and closes it.

Chapter 11

Lower Bend, Kentucky

*A*n old truck travels down a country road. Farm animals are grazing. Birds are singing. Ducks are swimming in a pond as Helen Wallace, now called Granny by everyone, drives by. She sees lots of wildflowers on the side of the road. The sunflowers are bigger than ever this year. Every so often a spray of dirt blows across the road.

Granny drives up to her faded little house. It's old looking, but the property is very clean. The long front porch is now a faded red. The stone chimney on the side of the house is a little sideways. The yard is mainly dirt except for a few trees and a few patches of grass. There is an old plow; a wheelbarrow full of flowers sits in the front yard. Tree stumps, used for makeshift chairs, are on the front porch. In the background are rolling hills. To the left and right of the house are winding pathways, bordered by stones. Even though the house is old, she has kept it up the best she can, and it's a beautiful place.

Granny parks the old, red Ford truck in the yard

and gets out; she has a rag in her hand. Dressed in a worn housedress, apron, brown shoes, and hose rolled down around her ankles, she looks older than her age. She walks over to a 1936 Ford coupe and starts polishing it. Thelma, her cat, comes up to her and rubs against her legs, seeking her attention. Granny ignores the cat and keeps on polishing the car. The car shines in the sunshine, so shiny that she can see her reflection on the hood. "God, I look awful. Oh well." She stands back to admire her work and gives the car one last look.

All of a sudden she hears a sneezing sound coming from inside her house. "God bless ya, Harry." Looking back at the hood of the car, she sees she missed a spot. She walks over, leans over the spot and breathes on it, then takes her polishing rag from her apron and rubs out the spot. Granny stands back, admiring the car, and smiles. She hears sounds of breaking glass coming from inside the house. Her expression changes to one of slight irritation. She throws down the polishing rag and heads toward the house, muttering to herself. "Darn you, Harry. What are you doing? Good for nothing ..."

Her rant against Harry is interrupted when the front door swings open. Maxie Johnson, a heavy-set, kindly black woman somewhere in her thirties, shows Harry, a billy goat, out the front door. In her deep Southern accent, Maxie says, "Good for nothin' is right."

Gianna, Granny's granddaughter, ten years old with dark, curly hair and big brown eyes, is right behind Maxie. Gianna, also with a Southern accent, says, "Don't be mean to Harry. You'll hurt his feelings."

Maxie and Granny can't help but laugh. Maxie looks at Granny. "We are heading down to the church to do some singing."

Granny replies, "Okay, but don't be late for supper. Black-eyed peas."

Gianna looks at her grandmother and makes a face; "Yuk!"

Granny gives Gianna a pat on the butt. "Never you mind, child. You just go learn some of those church songs." Granny smiles and shakes her head. "I love this child so much."

Chapter 12

The Pursuit

*J*ohnny, walking in a very dark area, looks from side to side to see if anyone is around. His steps become faster as he approaches a black van. He opens the back door of the van and, as fast as he can, puts a box inside. He walks around to the driver's side door, not too sure that no one has seen him. He gets in the van and lights up a cigarette. He sits there for a while, deep in thought. He takes a long drag off his cigarette, puts the van in gear, and pulls onto the street. He swings around the corner and onto another street. Still nervous, he pulls over and stops, and he takes another long drag off his cigarette. He sees the front end of a police car parked in an alley. His jaw drops; the cigarette falls in his lap. He turns off his headlights. He is scared; his hands shake; he doesn't move. From where he is parked, he can hear the police radio dispatcher loud and clear: 91 Adam. Code one. 1120 Burton Way, toy warehouse. 459 now. Suspect may be driving a black van. 91 Adam, responding.

Johnny squirms. He feels the cigarette burning on

his lap. He pulls out onto the street slowly, sweating profusely. He knows they will see him, and they do. Johnny picks up speed. The police car veers across the center line. Johnny's attention suddenly shifts from the burning cigarette to his side-view mirror, where he sees the police car speeding up and getting closer, lights flashing and siren wailing. He finds the lit cigarette and tosses it out the window. He curses under his breath: "Damn!" He pushes the gas pedal to the floor. He can hear his engine kick into gear. He speeds through one stop sign, then another. The police car takes the corner wide and screams up a different street. He hears the sirens in the distance; he has lost them for a minute. He keeps checking his rear-view mirror for any sight of the pursuer. He rounds the corner and turns in the opposite direction; he sees the red lights from the patrol car spin away from him through the dark road ahead.

The streets wind and climb. He speeds onward, the van moving dangerously fast. Suddenly a familiar viewpoint comes into sight. Johnny turns down a street and heads toward a big warehouse. A black overhead door opens and he pulls in fast, screeching to a stop. The door closes behind him. Johnny is scared and upset. He wipes the sweat off his forehead.

All of a sudden one of the other doors opens up and a black-and-white police car comes flying in. The large door closes. A cop jumps out of the car and walks toward the van, slamming his fist on the hood. Johnny sees the gold I.D. bracelet with the initials M.N. Johnny's friend from childhood, Mike Nessen, now a rugged-looking man in his late twenties, yells at Johnny. "You were in there for at least ten! What the hell were you doing tonight, daydreaming? I can only cover you for six minutes. You were in there for at least ten."

Johnny gets out of the van carrying a box and throws it to Mike. Mike catches the box with a step backward. Johnny gives Mike a dirty look.

"Mike, I want out."

"Out?"

"Yes, out. It was a close call tonight."

"It was only a close call because of your stupidity. Just remember, when your blood runs warm, it keeps you on your toes."

"Bullshit!"

Mike, getting mad, screams at Johnny. "Oh yeah. I almost forgot how much you hate everything, especially since you killed your wife and child."

Johnny explodes with anger and punches Mike in the jaw, knocking him to the floor. He then storms out of the warehouse.

Mike rubs his jaw and stares after Johnny with hate in his eyes as he watches him leave the warehouse.

Chapter 13

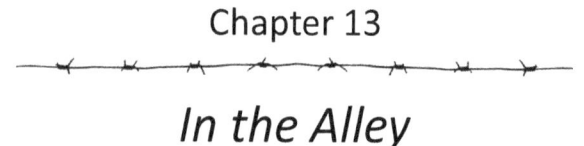

In the Alley

Johnny staggers through the dark alley; a few raindrops fall on his face. He is carrying a bottle of bourbon; he takes a drink and tilts back his head as he downs the last drop. He sees a hazy figure of an old man dressed in worn and tattered clothing and wearing a hood slowly walking toward him. Johnny thinks he sees something, but he's not sure. He closes his eyes, rubbing them, and shakes his head. He falls to the ground. The old man, now right in front of him, extends his hand to Johnny and helps him up. Johnny's mind goes back to the day on the church steps; he can tell it's the same old man from the church who is helping him up. He does indeed recognize the old man and is more scared than he was as a boy.

The old man speaks in a very soft voice. "The ring."

"What the …?"

The old man repeats. "Where is the ring?"

The old man pulls Johnny to his feet. Johnny is having trouble holding himself up straight. He collects his thoughts and almost stands at attention. Still not able to see the old man's face, Johnny stutters, "I ... I ... I don't know. I ... lost it." Johnny closes his eyes as if to close out the sound echoing through the night. The old man's voice is all he can hear.

"You must find it again. You must find it."

As the old man's voice trails off, Johnny opens his eyes. The sounds and the old man are gone. Johnny rubs his eyes again, wondering if he was dreaming or did this really happen. He composes himself and staggers on down the alley.

Chapter 14

Birthday!

Gianna and Granny are dusting and straightening up the house. Gianna is so excited because it's her birthday. Her dark eyes light up from the glow of the oil lamp. She cleans it very carefully. Granny gently says, "Be careful with the lamp." Gianna nods and moves over to where the wooden lion is sitting that Johnny made for his mom many years ago. Gianna carefully dusts the lion. Around the lion's neck is Johnny's ring on a chain.

"Where do you think my daddy is?"

"I don't know, honey. When your mother died, he was very upset and blamed himself for the accident. He took off … he thought both of you were gone to heaven."

"I wish he would come home."

"He just disappeared, and no one has seen or heard from him since."

"Was it his fault?" Gianna looks at Granny for answers.

"No, honey, it was a hit and run. Another car forced

him off the road and into a tree and didn't stop. They think he must have been drinking. There was nothing your father could do."

Gianna studies Granny for a moment. "Does he love me?"

"I'm sure if he knew you, there's no way he could not love you, just like I do." Granny smiles and goes over to Gianna and gives her a long hug.

"Is he ever coming back?"

"I sure hope he'll come back one day and find out he has a wonderful little daughter."

Granny moves on around the room dusting the furniture; she has a sad look on her face.

"You miss him?"

"Very much. I got sick after he left, and you were so little and cute and I didn't know what I was going to do, or how I was going to take care of you. So I had to sell our little house, because we needed the money. That's how I met Maxie. She came and took care of us. She gave us a place to live right here next to her."

Gianna, speaking loudly, says, "I love Maxie."

At that very moment Maxie appears at the screen door, looking in. "Did I hear my name?" Maxie most of the time has a smile on her face, a smile that could melt your heart, and jolly as Old Saint Nick. As Maxie enters the room, Gianna runs to give her a hug.

"Hi, honey child, what are you two doing?"

"Granny was just telling me about my daddy. You know, Maxie, if my daddy knew me, he would love me."

Maxie studies Gianna for a second. "I know he would, child."

Granny puts down her old dusting rag and looks at Gianna. "We have done enough work for one day, don't you think?"

"It's a special day, you know." Gianna can hardly contain her excitement.

"Oh, is it?" Maxie looks at Gianna and brings out a present from behind her back.

"You didn't forget?"

"How could I forget. You have reminded me every day on our walk from school."

Granny looks at Gianna. "You didn't."

"Well, I kinda did." Gianna takes the present and looks at Granny.

"Why don't you put the present on the table and you can open it after supper. I am sure Maxie will join us for supper." Maxie shakes her head yes. "Why don't you go out and play with Thelma so Maxie and I can set a spell."

Gianna hands her dusting rag to Granny and runs toward the door. "Okay. I will go and play with Thelma." Out the screen door she goes, running as fast as she can.

Granny starts to say "Don't slam the ..." as the

screen door slams shut. She smiles as she watches Gianna go out toward the big locust tree. Thelma is already there waiting for her.

Maxie shakes her head. "She is some child, isn't she."

Granny, somewhat daydreaming, replies, "She is a very special child, and to think how she came into this world."

Granny goes over to the table where the carved lion is. She takes the ring off and holds it in her hands for a moment, then holds it to her heart as if saying a silent prayer as she looks up to the ceiling. She hangs the ring back around the lion's neck. Looking at Maxie, she says softly, "I remember it as if it were yesterday when Johnny gave me that lion on Christmas morning. Took him a year to finish it, whittling on it every chance he got, and then it was Christmas morning. He had it wrapped in some old newspaper. He was so proud of himself that he got it finished in time for Christmas. Of course, the best present was that his leg was healed and he could walk. I cried day and night, thanking God for the miracle. It was the best present we got." Granny has tears in her eyes, and so does Maxie.

"It's nice to have somebody to love, isn't it," Maxie says quietly.

Granny snaps out of her temporary trance and turns to Maxie, who is now sitting in one of the rocking chairs. "Maxie?"

"Yes, ma'am?"

Granny goes over and gives Maxie a hug. "I so appreciate you and all you have done for us." She then looks Maxie straight in the eye. "You have been waiting for years for Frank to come home. Think he's ever coming?"

Maxie doesn't say anything for a few moments. "I don't know. All I can do is hope, dream, and pray. The good Lord knows I have plenty of time for praying. You know, I look down that old dirt road every day, hoping my man will come back. Not even a speck of dust or a letter."

Maxie and Granny don't know Gianna snuck back in the house and is sitting in the corner, listening to them talk.

"You think he may have got into some kind of trouble?"

Maxie answers quickly. "Not my Frank. He was a fine Christian man, he was."

"What, then."

"We just had a little quarrel and I said something, you know, something I shouldn't have said, something about his mother. I meant no harm by it, but before I could apologize, he packed his bag and off he went home to his mammy."

"Did you guys get along?"

"Lord yes. We did everything together. Why, he

couldn't even use that old outhouse unless I waited outside. Spoiled him rotten, I did."

"But that was years ago, Maxie."

"I know. That little quarrel seems so unimportant now. Lord, I don't even remember what I said."

Maxie stands up from the rocking chair and reaches into the pocket of her faded blue dress and takes out an old quarter. Looking down at it, she rubs it in her hand for a few moments, then flips it up in the air and catches it. "You know, it seems like only yesterday that Frank and I were walking down that road out there when this here quarter flipped up out of nowhere and landed in his shirt pocket. It scared him almost to death at first, and I laughed 'cause nothing ever scared old Frank."

"That same quarter?"

"Yeah. He thought it must have come from heaven. So he gave it to me. Said it must be some kind of a good luck piece, maybe it would come in handy someday."

Granny takes the quarter from Maxie's hand to get a better look at it, and hands it back to Maxie.

"I guess this here quarter makes me feel like a part of him is still here. Do you understand?"

Gianna, still sitting on the floor, is half listening to their conversation and half dozing off.

"I understand, Maxie. Look at me and that old car of Johnny's. Why, I should have gotten rid of it long ago. Lord knows we could use the money. But it's a part of me that still holds his memory alive, and hope that one day he will return."

Gianna wakes up. "Get rid of who, old Frank?"

Granny and Maxie look to where she is sitting. They both are surprised to see her.

Granny scolds Gianna. "You do not say old Frank. You must respect your elders."

Gianna shrugs her shoulders. "Sorry. I just thought listening to Maxie that he is old."

Chapter 15

Los Angeles Warehouse

 *J*ohnny leans against his car, a 1937 Studebaker. Shavings are all over the ground from the piece of wood he is whittling. Rod, a young, clean-cut man, definitely not your criminal-looking type, walks up to Johnny.

"What you doin', man?"

"Who wants to know?"

"Mike's lookin' for ya."

Johnny is not in a good mood. "What does he want?"

"Double checking the schedule, I guess."

"It's not even dark yet."

"Well, you know Mike."

"Too well. All my life."

"What's eatin' ya, man?"

"What do you mean?"

"I mean you're not yourself." Rod fidgets nervously.

Johnny looks down at his ring finger. He is still whittling and not paying much attention to Rod. He notices Rod's behavior. "Are you nervous?"

"I just want to get this over with. I have a big date tonight."

"You've been having that big date for the past three years." Johnny notices that Rod tenses up a little with his remark. He stops whittling and looks straight into Rod's eyes. "How old are you?"

Rod looks at Johnny, a little confused. "I just turned twenty last week."

"Why don't you get out of here and get a real job?"

"Why don't you?"

Before they can say another word, they hear Mike in the other room calling their names. Rod and Johnny just look at each other. Johnny puts the wood and knife in the car and they both start walking toward Mike.

Mike is in street clothes, not in his uniform. Johnny feels bothered and indecisive as he walks toward Mike.

"Hey hothead, is your fist sore?"

Johnny shakes his head no.

Rubbing his face, Mike continues. "Well, my jaw is. Got a new job for you." He points to a new, dark blue van. "See that van? It's filled with toys now and you are driving it to Nashville."

"Nashville? Why Nashville?"

"Because I have a man there who will pay a lot of money for these toys."

"So what kind of toys?"

"You don't need to know. All I need you to do is drive it there and fly back to Los Angeles. Since you don't celebrate holidays, you might as well stay busy."

"No! I can't do it. I came here only to tell you I want out."

Mikes laughs. "You can't get out until I say you're out, get it? Remember, you owe me."

"Owe you for what? Making me a crook?"

Mike gets a little loud. "For keeping you out of jail. I could have run you in that night I caught you at that liquor store. Remember?"

"I wasn't doing anything and you know that. I was just at the wrong place at the wrong time."

Mike's temper flares. "If I hadn't saved your butt that night you would be in jail with the rest of the Harley Gang."

"I wasn't with them and you know it!"

"Yeah. Tell that to the judge. Just like you're doin' nothin' now? You could be rotting in prison if it wasn't for me."

Johnny gives Mike a dirty look. Mike puts his arm around Johnny's shoulder and starts walking him toward the van. "Still haven't decided what you want to grow up to be, have you, Johnny?"

"Maybe not. It's like when we were kids playing cops and robbers, you always played the bad guy. I didn't know which one to play."

"Be like me. Play them both. Works for me."

"Until we get caught."

"Me get caught? I don't think so, Johnny."

"It'll happen one day, pal, your luck will not always be with you."

Mike puts the keys in Johnny's hand. Johnny starts walking away, then turns and looks back at Mike.

Sarcastically, Mike sends him off. "Good luck. Instructions are in the glove box. See you in about ten days, and be careful. A lot of money riding on this load."

Johnny looks at Mike for a few moments and then walks out of the warehouse to his car. Mike hollers after him, "Don't be late tomorrow," and watches him leave.

Chapter 16

A Good Deed

*I*t's late afternoon in a rundown neighborhood. A shiny red Dodge truck pulls up in front of an apartment building. Two teenage boys are in the truck. The driver, Tony, honks the horn. Jose, a young Mexican teenager, comes out of the apartment building and walks over to the car.

Tony nods at Jose. "Can you take a look at the engine? It's missing."

"Sure." Jose walks to the front of the truck and opens the hood. He starts to check the wires and hoses. After a few minutes Danny, the other teenager in the truck, puts his head out the window.

"Hey, asshole, hurry it up! We've got some hot chicks waiting for us. Something you would know nothing about."

Jose gets out from under the hood of the truck and stands to the side. "Try it now."

Tony turns the key and the engine roars. "Thanks! Maybe I'll let you drive this someday. Now out of my way."

Danny chimes in. "But don't hold your breath."

Danny and Tony laugh as they drive away.

At that moment Johnny pulls up to the curb; he watches the truck pulling away, screeching the tires. He exits the Studebaker that he picked up cheap from a little old lady he met at the grocery store.

"They giving you a hard time again, Jose?"

"It's okay, Mr. Johnny, I don't let them get to me."

"Are you sure?"

Jose just looks at Johnny. "I put your mail on the table and took Goldie for a walk."

Johnny reaches in his pocket and gives Jose some money.

"Could I wash your car, Mr. Johnny?"

Johnny throws him the keys. "Be my guest."

Johnny goes into his apartment. The mail, lots of it, is stacked on the table. He looks at it, piece by piece, and throws each one in the wastebasket, unopened. He comes to one letter and stares at it for a few minutes. The letter is addressed to Helen Wallace, 125 Meridian Street, Lower Bend, Kentucky. He rubs his finger over the address. It's stamped with "No forwarding address—return to sender" in big red letters. A tear runs down his face. He tosses the letter into the wastebasket along with the junk mail and heads to bed.

The next morning, after having a bad night, Johnny gulps down the last bit of coffee and exits the apartment, carrying a suitcase. The sun is so bright that he pulls his sunglasses out of his shirt pocket and puts them on. Goldie, his Golden Retriever, is right behind him. He stops in his tracks and stares in amazement. He walks over to his car, now washed, waxed, and shining like new in the morning sun. Jose, a big smile on his face, stands in the background and watches Johnny with excitement.

Jose walks over to the car. "You like, Mr. Johnny?"

Johnny is shocked and shakes his head. "You are a genius. I don't know how you do it."

Goldie barks, as in agreement. Johnny and Jose bend down and hug Goldie; she barks again.

"Jose, I need a favor."

"Anything, Mr. Johnny."

"Hop in the car."

Goldie jumps in the back seat. Johnny drives toward the warehouse. He pulls over and parks in the warehouse parking lot. He turns and looks at Jose.

"Is everything okay, Mr. Johnny?"

Johnny waits a moment. "Jose, I've got to go on a long trip, a very long trip. I want to make you a deal."

"A deal, Mr. Johnny? I don't understand."

"Well, it's like this. I may never come back here again. There are some unfinished things I need to do. I can't explain, you just need to trust me. I want you to keep the car. I'm giving it to you. The paperwork is in the glove compartment."

"This car?"

"Yes. In turn, you must take care of Goldie. She is your dog now."

"I still don't understand."

"I don't expect you to. Just trust me and don't tell anyone we had this conversation."

"Okay, Mr. Johnny, my lips are sealed."

Johnny gets out of the car. He gives Goldie a long hug; she licks the tears that run down his face. "Goodbye, girl." Goldie looks at him as if she knows it's goodbye. Johnny walks around to the passenger side of the car. Jose, just sitting there, looks at Johnny. "Hey. I know you are a genius with cars, but I don't think you can drive from this side."

Jose jumps out of the car. Johnny gives him a handshake, then gives him a hug as an afterthought. "Get in. The keys are in the ignition."

"Are you sure about this, Mr. Johnny?"

"Very sure. Take care of yourself and Goldie." Goldie whines.

"Mr. Johnny, someone might think I stole this car."

"Like I said, it's all yours. The pink slip is in the glove compartment."

"Thank you, Mr. Johnny."

"No, thank you. Now get out of here and take care of yourself and Goldie."

Jose stares at Johnny for a moment, then pulls away.

Chapter 17

At the Farm

*M*eanwhile, back in Kentucky, Gianna is outside the outhouse. She is dancing around like she needs to go to the bathroom. She turns toward the outhouse door. "Granny ... I've got to go!" No one answers. "Granny ... I've really got to go." Still no one answers. "Granny, never you mind, I am going in the bushes."

Granny grumbles from inside the outhouse. "All right, all right ... I'm comin'."

Gianna giggles, holding her hands over her mouth, trying to be quiet.

Granny exits the outhouse. "What's so funny?"

"I was only joking."

"Why, you little stinker, I'll get you." Granny starts chasing Gianna down the lane, both giggling with joy.

The next morning Gianna exits the house, school books and lunch in hand. Granny, in the house behind the screen door, waves goodbye.

"Have a good day, and don't be lollygagging on the way." She knows Gianna will stop and talk to every critter she sees and will be late for school.

Gianna walks down the dirt road and waves goodbye to Granny. As she walks out of sight, she turns to make sure Granny can't see her. She sees Thelma sunning herself. She bends down to pet the cat. "Good morning, Thelma. Did you sleep well?" Suddenly she hears Granny's voice.

"I have eyes in the back of my head. Get going or you will be late for school."

Gianna takes her time and sees Harry grazing on the grass.

"I can see you!"

"I'm going, Granny!"

Gianna walks on down the road. She stops for a few seconds to take a look at a squirrel, who takes a few moments away from chewing the nuts and looks toward her. "Hi, Mr. Brownie, how are you today?"

She continues walking, though slowly, looking at the birds and butterflies flying around some flowers. She comes upon a crow that has its foot caught in some wire. She bends down and frees the crow. "There now, Mr. Crow, you are fine now." The crow flies away. She seems so proud of herself and continues on. She comes upon a deer, who walks over to her. You can tell by the friendliness of the deer that this is a regular daily meeting. Gianna pats the deer on the head and gives her a hug. "Good morning, Maggie." She looks at the small watch on her wrist and starts to run down the road to try to get to school on time.

Maxie goes to the school every afternoon to walk Gianna home. They skip along together and sing songs. Maxie's beautiful voice resonates through the peaceful countryside. Butterflies fly around them and land on the flowers.

"It's a beautiful day," Maxie exclaims. "The clouds are high in the sky. We are happy to be alive."

"We sure are, and I am happy to be out of school."

Maxie laughs and shakes her head. "Did you learn anything today?"

"Not too much. I got to go back tomorrow."

Back at the house, Granny is gathering some wood from a pile near the house. She hears the singing and looks up, smiling as their voices become louder.

"That doesn't sound like any church hymn I ever heard."

"I learned some new songs, Granny."

"Well, that's nice, I guess."

"Want to hear one?"

"Sure do."

Gianna looks at Maxie to see what to do next. Maxie coaches her. "Remember what I taught you, now."

Maxie and Gianna start to sing. Maxie starts it off, and Gianna comes in.

"We are looking at the sky, the clouds are high, we're dancing along the highway ..."

They do gestures with their hands and do a

little soft-shoe. They are quite charming. Granny is impressed. As they finish their song, Granny claps her hands. She joins in and does a little soft-shoe herself. They all begin to laugh.

Chapter 18

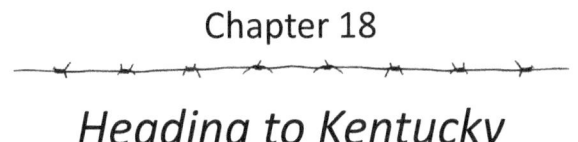

Heading to Kentucky

 *J*ohnny drives the van down the highway; he slows down with the other cars as they approach a toll booth. Since he is stopped in traffic, he reads the road signs ahead. He is headed to Nashville. Nashville angles off to the left and Ashland angles off to the right. Johnny takes his toll booth ticket and heads to the right toward Ashland, Kentucky.

Chapter 19

That Old Car

*G*ranny, out in the yard, dusts off the car again. Gianna helps with a little polishing rag, just like her Granny's larger one. Something is on her mind. "Granny?"

"Yes, child?"

"Why haven't you taken me for a ride in Dad's old car?"

"Good question. The battery is dead."

Gianna smiles. "Good reason."

Granny looks at her sweet little face. "Well, come on. We'll pretend."

Granny and Gianna throw down the polishing rags and jump into the car. Gianna gets into the driver's seat. She pretends to start the car and turns the steering wheel back and forth. As she begins making "car sounds" a loud thunderclap makes them almost jump out of their skin. They both can't stop laughing.

"Lord, that almost scared me to death."

Gianna, mimicking Granny, says, "Lord, me too."

Granny looks at Gianna seriously. "Gianna, are you

happy out here? I mean, do you wish we still lived in town?"

Gianna, perking up, replies, "You mean like my friend Bobbie Jo does?"

"Yes, honey … like your friend Bobbie Jo does."

Gianna looks puzzled. "Are we moving?"

Granny, still sitting in the passenger seat of the car, straightens Gianna's hair. "No, honey. I just wondered how you felt about living in the city."

Gianna lays her head on Granny's shoulder. "I like living out here in the country with you and Maxie."

"So you don't miss having no friends to play with?"

Gianna sits up straight and puts her hands on the steering wheel again. She looks over at Granny. "Shucks no. I have Thelma, Harry, Brownie, and Maggie."

Granny smiles at her. "But they are all animals."

"I know, and I love them. It's noisy in town, Granny. All the birds fly away. And the animals need me. And who would take care of them if I wasn't here?"

"Well, I guess you have a point. You're the best granddaughter in the world."

"And you're the best Granny."

Granny likes that. "You are absolutely right."

Chapter 20

Welfare Officers

*G*ranny and Gianna are sitting on the porch. Granny is in her rocking chair. She has a tea-towel over her lap with string beans in it; she snaps the beans and throws them in a pot on the porch floor. Gianna pets Thelma the cat and laughs at the sound of the beans dropping in the pot.

A young man, tall and slender, dressed in a suit that is way too warm for such a hot summer day in the South, walks up to Granny and Gianna. At the same time an older, matronly type woman comes up by the side of the house. She walks into the yard and over to Granny and Gianna.

Startled, Granny and Gianna scream, scaring the two intruders, who scream also, stepping back a few feet. Granny collects herself quickly.

The woman looks at Granny. "Are you Helen Wallace?"

Granny is not pleased. "Who wants to know?"

"I am Alice Jones and this is Kevin Hughes. We are from the Social Services office."

"Social Services?"

"Better known to you folks probably as the welfare office."

Granny looks at Alice and very sarcastically replies. "Oh really? Well, for your information, Mrs. Jones, I've never set foot in any welfare office in my life."

"Is that so ..."

Kevin breaks into the conversation. "We are really here because we heard you have a little girl living out here."

Gianna takes notice and just stares at them both.

"Yes, you are looking at her. She is my granddaughter."

"Well, we are here to check out how the child is living."

Granny is mad at what Alice just said. "She's living like any other child."

Kevin butts in. "Are there any other children around? Maybe some colored children?"

"For your information, we don't discuss the color of someone's skin in this neck of the woods. But if there were any colored children, as you put it, Gianna would be happy to play with them."

Alice looks around to see if she can see or hear any other children.

"To answer your question, no other children live out here."

Alice continues the questioning. "What about

her school?"

"What about her school? She goes to Lower Bend Elementary. And I might add she is a straight-A student."

"And of course you drive her every day."

"But of course."

Alice tries her best to trick Granny. "Who does the child play with? I mean, who are her best friends out here?"

"She makes friends with everyone, especially the animals."

Alice reacts disgustedly as Thelma rubs up against her legs. Granny motions for Thelma to move. Thelma meows and moves away. "The animals?"

Kevin butts in again. "What about her mother and father?"

Granny by now is getting really mad and her patience is running low, but she tries to keep cool. "What is all this about?"

"Our job is to make sure the child is being properly cared for."

Now Alice butts in. "Where are her parents?"

"Her mother died in an accident, and her father ... is ... is ... away on business."

"We have heard rumors that he's been gone since the child was born."

"Well, that just goes to show you can't believe rumors, doesn't it? Now if I could just show you the way to the road."

Alice doesn't want Granny to get in the last word or get the best of her. "When will Mr. Wallace, your son ..."

Granny cuts her off. "Right."

"... be back?"

"A week or two."

"Fine. You won't mind us talking to him when he returns?"

Granny glares at both of them. "Not at all. Now if you don't mind, I have work to do."

"Thank you for your time."

Alice and Kevin head toward the road. "She is lying, Kevin."

"You don't know that."

Alice looks around the farm. "They all lie. I'm checking the records to see how much money she is getting."

"She said she wasn't getting any money."

"We'll see, and we'll take that child out of this place and give her a nice home." Alice stops and looks around once more. "There's probably a dozen of them black children hiding out there. And just look at this place."

"Personally, I think it's quite nice and peaceful out here. I grew up in a place like this and I turned out okay."

Alice gives Kevin a dirty look as she motions him to get into their car. They pull away.

Chapter 21

A Scam?

*M*axie is walking toward the house as Alice and Kevin drive by. Alice gives Maxie the eye. "Just look at that. Who is that colored lady anyway?"

"Looks like she lives next door."

"In that nice house? I doubt it. They're probably all running a scam on the welfare office. I'll get to the bottom of this and have that child put in a foster home."

"Don't you think you are taking this too far? A foster home? She looks like she is loved and cared for to me."

Alice is steaming mad. "What do you know. Just drive."

Chapter 22

At the Cemetery

Johnny drives into the town of Lower Bend, Kentucky. He looks around at all the various shops. His eye catches the Lower Bend Soda Shoppe. He smiles as he passes by, remembering better times and how often he and Priscilla spent time there, drinking sodas.

A strange look crosses his face as he sees a sign for the cemetery. He makes a sharp turn and heads there. He pulls over, stops, and exits the van. He walks among the tombstones, searching. He takes out his knife and opens the blade close to his face, then closes it. He opens the knife again and once more holds it close to his face. It sparkles as the sun shines bright against the blade. He walks toward an object. He stops and bends down, and his expression changes again. The blade still shining in the sun, he draws it back and brings it down to cut a beautiful red rose from a bush that is growing in the cemetery. He picks up the rose and smells it. Tears roll down his face as he slowly lays the rose on a grave.

He reaches up to the tombstone and runs his fingers over the writing. He reads the inscription out loud as he touches each word: "Priscilla Wallace. Beloved wife of John Wallace. May our hearts beat as one." Suddenly he hears a child's voice behind him.

"Daddy? Daddy?"

Johnny jumps and turns toward the voice. A young woman around twenty-five holds a large bundle of flowers in one hand, the hand of a little girl in the other. Embarrassed, she looks down at the child. "Shhh. He's not your daddy." She looks over at Johnny; he stares back at her. A tear rolls down his cheek. The woman speaks softly. "I am so sorry." They stare at each other for a second, as if they both understand the pain. She turns and walks deeper into the cemetery.

Chapter 23

Harry

Gianna plays with Harry the goat by the rear end of an old car. She sits on the ground and Harry stands next to her. Maxie walks into the yard toward them and stops by the car. Gianna, unaware that anyone is around, talks to Harry. "Do you have a daddy?" Harry makes a BLAAA sound. "I mean, a real daddy." Gianna looks into Harry's eyes. "I have a real daddy."

Maxie, listening to this, has a sad look on her face. She walks over to Gianna and Harry and touches Gianna's arm. "Are you talking to Harry?"

"Uh huh."

"What did he say?"

"Harry can't talk. He's just a good listener." Gianna, with sad eyes, looks at Maxie. "Will my daddy come back some day?"

"I'm almost sure he will."

"Granny misses him so much."

"I know she does, child."

"And I want to meet him when he comes back and see if he loves me."

"He loves you now; he just doesn't know it yet. I have this feeling deep inside me that he will be home soon."

"I touch his lucky ring every day and make a wish. Granny says it only glows for him." Gianna pauses. "I know you want old Frank to come home and you have that lucky quarter … for a stamp."

Maxie looks at her for a moment, a little puzzled.

"That lucky quarter he gave you. Now you write to old Frank. Gotta make you own luck, Maxie."

Gianna's words make Maxie think; it sinks in. She gives Gianna a big hug. "Oh honey, you're so right. I have waited too long. I will write that letter tonight!" Maxie takes the old quarter out of her pocket and looks down at it. "Gotta make your own luck! You go get cleaned up. We'll go into town and visit Bobbie Jo. Would you like that?"

"Yes! I will go tell Granny."

Chapter 24

Looking for Mother

*J*ohnny, inside a phone booth, puts a lot of change in the phone and begins to dial. An operator's voice says, "The number you have called has been disconnected. There is no new number." Johnny hangs up the phone and collects the returned change. A puzzled look on his face, he begins feeding the change back into the phone. "Operator, do you have a listing for a Helen Wallace on Meridian Street? ... Are you sure?" He slams down the phone. He gets back into his van and slowly drives down Meridian Street, stopping in front of a beautifully kept white house. He stares at the house for a few minutes and reads the house number out loud: "125 Meridian." He exits the van and slowly walks up to the door and knocks. A lady in her mid-thirties opens the door.

"Umm ... hi, I'm looking for Helen Wallace."

"I'm sorry, no Helen Wallace lives here."

"I know she used to. Maybe you bought the house from her?"

"No, actually it was in probate. The owner had

died." Johnny steps back, surprise and sadness crossing his face. "Are you okay?"

"Oh ... yes ... I'm sorry I bothered you."

"No bother at all. I'm sorry I couldn't help you."

Johnny turns and walks back toward the van. He stops by the mailbox and bends down to inspect the post. He finds the names he carved long ago: Johnny Loves Priscilla.

Chapter 25

Granny Makes a Dress

*G*ranny sits at her old sewing machine, sewing away on a brightly colored flowered dress. The screen door slams shut as Gianna walks in from outside. "Child, will you not slam that door?"

"Sorry. Is it ready yet?"

"Just one minute." Granny stops sewing, pulls the fabric out from under the needle, puts it up to her mouth, and bites off the thread. She stands up and turns around, holding a small dress in front of her. She gives Gianna the eye. "Well, what do you think?"

"I think it's beautiful. But Granny, could I have a store-boughten dress sometime?"

"Get over here and try this dress on." Granny helps Gianna put on the dress and turns her around so she can button the back, then turns her back around to see how it looks on her. Granny is pleased with it. She gives Gianna a kiss on the cheek. "You don't need a store-bought one. I made you a beautiful dress. Why, just look at you ... pretty as a doll."

Gianna smiles. "I know."

Granny smiles at Gianna's remark and gives her a pat on the butt. "Now go outside, child, and play while I get ready."

"I will go out and play with Thelma and Harry."

"But don't get dirty before we leave."

"I won't. I promise."

Maxie enters the house as Gianna leaves to play outside. Gianna greets her. "I am going to have fun today playing with Bobbie Jo."

"I know you will have a fun day, and you look so pretty."

"I know I do."

Maxie shakes her head. "You better get out in that yard before I change my mind."

Granny puts away all her sewing needs. "I want you to let me off at the courthouse today for a while, Maxie."

"Anything you need, Miss Wallace?"

"I want to do some checking on my legal rights."

"You mean those welfare people who came out here?"

"Right. The nerve of those two thinking I don't take good care of Gianna!" Sarcasm sweeps into her voice. "Is there any colored children around?"

"Don't get yourself upset. Maybe they were more concerned about the color of my skin ..."

Granny interrupts. "Well it ain't right, Maxie! Why, if it hadn't been for you taking care of us like you did when I got sick, I would have lost all my savings, and where would we be today?"

"Now Miss Wallace, don't you fret none about me and get yourself all upset."

"I'm not, Maxie, but it makes me so darn mad. Why, I helped put Lower Bend on the map. I still know some good stories about Mayor Brown, if you know what I mean."

Maxie chuckles. "I sure do, Miss Wallace. But why did you tell them Johnny would be home in two weeks?"

"I didn't know what to say. That woman had me so flustered."

"God works in mysterious ways. Maybe he will be home."

"I sure hope so. I pray on that ring of his every night." Granny walks over to where the lion is sitting on the table. Johnny's ring, on a chain, hangs around the lion's neck. She picks up the ring and touches it softly. "Who knows. Maybe by some miracle, maybe he will come home. You know, the other night I thought I saw the ring glow for a few seconds." Granny lets go of the ring and picks up her sweater, which is lying close by.

When Granny is not looking, Gianna comes back into the house to get her sweater. She takes the chain and ring off the lion and puts it around her neck.

Chapter 26

Going to Town

$\mathcal{A}$ Chrysler drives by a lush green field where Guernsey cows are grazing. It winds its way around some turns and finally reaches a small town. Granny and Maxie are there to check out the stores. Gianna is asleep in the back seat. Maxie, who is driving, pulls over to the curb and parks.

Gianna wakes up. "Can I get some ice cream?"

"Why don't we all get some ice cream," Granny suggests.

As they come out of the ice cream shop, Granny turns to Maxie. "I won't be long, Maxie." She then turns to Gianna. "You mind your manners, young lady, and play nice with Bobbie Jo."

"I will," Gianna promises.

"What time should I pick you up, Miss Wallace?"

"A couple of hours should be enough time."

Gianna sticks her head out of the car window. "Love you."

Granny bends down and gives her a kiss. "Love you too."

She turns and heads down the street toward the courthouse. Maxie pulls away from the curb and proceeds down the street.

Chapter 27

In the Neighborhood

*J*ohnny drives around the neighborhood, the same neighborhood as Maxie and Gianna. Maxie drives up to a stop sign, stops, looks in both directions, and turns right. At that moment, Johnny drives up to the same intersection, looks in both directions, and turns left.

Johnny drives down the street. He pulls the van over to the curb and stares at the neighborhood, trying to get his thoughts straight. He turns his radio on and taps to the beat of the music with both hands on the steering wheel. He stares up ahead and sees a green light way in the distance. He goes into a trance, remembering himself as a young boy as the old man put the ring on his finger. The sound of a horn honking brings him back to reality. He lights up a cigarette, takes a few puffs, and pulls back onto the street.

Granny walks down the sidewalk as Johnny drives by. He looks from side to side of the street. Just as he goes by Granny, she walks into a store, mere seconds before Johnny looks her way. He drives on down the street and out of sight.

Chapter 28

Playing with Bobbie Jo

*B*obbie Jo lives in a big white, two-story house. Maxie and Mrs. Wilson sit on the wrap-around porch having a glass of iced tea. Maxie rocks the glass back and forth. Bobbie Jo, a little colored girl who is nine years old, has a long braid hanging down her back. She is the same size as Gianna. Bobbie Jo and Gianna play in the yard with Bobbie Jo's small puppy. They throw a ball; the puppy runs after it. The two girls, laughing, try to beat the puppy to the ball. The ball bounces into the street, with the puppy and Gianna right behind it.

Johnny drives down the street, looking at every house, trying to see something he can relate to. His attention elsewhere, he doesn't see the puppy run across the street. Gianna sees the car is not going to stop; she dashes into the street to save the puppy. She and the puppy clear the van and make it to the other side of the street unharmed. With all the commotion, Gianna realizes the chain on her neck has broken and her father's ring is lying in the middle of the street.

She dashes back into the street to save it.

Johnny looks up and sees the little girl right in front of his van. He tries to swerve to miss her, but it's too late. He sees Gianna's lifeless body lying on the pavement. Johnny exits the van, picks up Gianna, and carries her to the yard. Maxie runs into the street, screaming. "Please, someone call an ambulance! Call the police!"

Johnny looks at the little girl, then at the van. He realizes he's in trouble; he runs to the van, gets in, and drives down the street and out of sight.

Maxie screams at him. "Come back here! You can't leave."

Chapter 29

The Emergency Room

Gianna is in the emergency room, lying still in the hospital bed. All kinds of monitors are hooked up to her small body. Doctor Baker and a nurse check the monitors and her pulse. After they finish, they look at her for a few moments. Dr. Baker shakes his head. "Let me know if there's any change."

"I will, Doctor."

Dr. Baker leaves the room and goes to the waiting room, where Granny and Maxie are anxiously waiting. He walks over to them. "Miss Wallace?"

"Yes?"

"She's still unconscious, but there are no broken bones, no internal bleeding. Only scrapes and bruises."

"Is she going to be alright?"

"We will know more by tomorrow. A nurse will be with her all night, and I can be reached anytime."

"I'll stay with her."

"No, you get some rest. Like I said, we will have a nurse with her around the clock. We do have a room for you so you can be right next door if you want to stay."

"Thank you. I would."

"Don't worry, Miss Wallace. She will be okay. Oh, I almost forgot." Reaching into her purse, Maxie takes out the ring on the broken chain and hands it to Granny. "This is what she ran out in the street to get."

"She had this on?"

"I guess she did."

"That is not like her to take the ring without my permission. Why, this has hung in the house for years. Wonder why today she decided to wear it?"

Chapter 30

Nashville Warehouse

*J*ohnny drives down a highway until he sees a sign that reads Nashville, Tennessee. He pulls off the freeway, goes down an alley, stops and backs up to an open warehouse door. Two guys take the merchandise out of the van. A middle-aged man, Louis, walks up to Johnny and hands him a fat envelope.

"I need the van for a few more days."

"No problem. Keep it as long as you want. They all got busted in Los Angeles, including your pal Mike."

Showing no reaction, Johnny replies, "He was not a pal of mine. That's what happens when you play cops and robbers."

"I have a feeling I won't be seeing you again. Good luck."

"Thanks, Louis. You won't, believe me."

Johnny leaves the warehouse and drives miles out of town. He veers off down a deserted highway and then off onto a dirt road, ending up at the edge of a cliff. He sits in the van for a few minutes to collect his thoughts. He gets out of the van, takes it out of park, goes to the back of the van, and pushes it over the cliff. It immediately bursts into flames. He watches the van burn as dark smoke rolls up, until nothing is left but some metal.

Johnny walks all the way back to the highway and starts to hitchhike. A semi stops, Johnny gets in, and they speed on down the road. When they come into the next town, the driver drops Johnny off at a used car lot. He buys a car and heads to Kentucky.

Chapter 31

Johnny Returns

$\mathcal{M}$axie pulls up in front of the hospital and stops. Granny exits the car and walks into the hospital. She walks down the hall and out of sight. Johnny is right behind her and walks up to the information desk. A clerk, busy behind the desk, looks up. "May I help you?"

"Where's your personnel office?"

"Down the hall, second door on the right."

"Thank you, ma'am."

Johnny gets a job at the hospital and is immediately put to work. Wearing work clothes, his hospital badge reading Housekeeping, he pushes a mop bucket down the hall and into an office. He looks around; no one else is in the room. He noses around the office and looks through some papers. Then he sees a file marked New Admissions. He goes through the file until he finds what he is looking for. He starts to read it when Miss Porter, a nurse, enters the room. Johnny drops the file on the floor and then acts like he's trying to pick up all of the paper that has fallen out.

The nurse gives him a dirty look.

"What are you doing?"

"I ... I ... I just dropped the file on the floor."

"I can see that. What are you doing in this room?"

"I thought there was a cleanup in here."

Miss Porter glances around the room. "Well, do you see anything to clean up?" She goes over to Johnny and takes the file out of his hand, then puts it back where it belongs.

Johnny is somewhat embarrassed, but he makes a little eye contact with her. "Sorry, I guess I got the wrong room."

Miss Porter sees that he is embarrassed. She calms down and replies softly, "I guess so."

Johnny pushes the mop bucket to the door and looks back at her. Miss Porter just stares at him and then gives him a slight smile as he exits the room.

Granny walks down the hall and comes to the Intensive Care Unit. It is night, and she has been crying. She slowly pushes open the door and walks into the room. Gianna's eyes are closed, and she is lying very still. She is hooked up to a few monitors. Granny walks over to her bedside and takes Gianna's little hand in hers. She whispers, "Gianna ... Gianna. It's Granny." Gianna lies still. No movement. "Gianna, can you hear me?"

Dr. Baker walks into the room and over to where Granny is standing. He touches her shoulder. Tears rolling down her cheeks, Granny looks at him. "Is she going to be okay?"

"I'm ordering more tests. We can't be sure yet." Miss Porter walks into the room. "Could you take Miss Wallace to the waiting room and get her anything she needs?"

"Of course. Miss Wallace, come with me." She puts her arm around Granny and walks her out of the room. They go to a nice waiting room where Maxie is sitting.

Maxie puts her arm around Granny. "Don't worry, Miss Wallace. She is in God's hands and she will be fine." Granny shakes her head yes. Miss Porter comes back in with two cups of coffee and hands them to Maxie and Granny.

Johnny comes down the hall by the waiting room, still pushing the mop bucket, but he doesn't look into the room. He slowly continues down the hall, looking in every small window trying to find the little girl. He comes upon one where he sees a small child lying in the bed. As he pushes against the door to go in, the door swings open and a nurse exits, almost hitting Johnny in the face. "We need a cleanup in there."

Johnny walks slowly into the room. He stares at Gianna's still body for a few moments, then he slowly walks over to her bedside. He looks down at her sadly. "I'm so sorry. Please forgive me." At that moment the nurse returns to the room.

"Did you clean up the spill?"

Johnny nervously looks around the room. He hurries to clean up the wet floor and quickly walks out of the room.

Chapter 32

Miss Porter

*J*ohnny sits by himself at a long table in the cafeteria, staring off into the distance, deep in thought. Miss Porter enters the cafeteria and spots Johnny sitting there alone. She picks up two cups of coffee and heads over to where he is sitting. Johnny did not see her come into the cafeteria and is a little startled as she sets the two cups on the table.

"Could I buy you a coffee?"

This takes Johnny by surprise. "Oh … uh … yes. Thank you."

Miss Porter sits down across from Johnny and smiles. "I'm sorry I was so rude tonight. You're new here, aren't you?"

"That's okay. Yes, I am new."

Miss Porter extends her hand to Johnny. "So I would like to start over. I'm Ambra Porter."

Johnny extends his hand. "Johnny. I'm Johnny … um … Johnny Brown."

"It's nice to meet you, Johnny Brown." She notices a sadness in his face. "Is there something wrong?"

Johnny fishes for what he should say next. "I just did a cleanup in room 431."

Miss Porter studies him for a moment. "I see. The little girl, Gianna ..."

Johnny interrupts. "Gianna?"

"Her name is Gianna. I'm in Pediatrics. It was a hit and run accident."

Johnny tries to hide his feelings of guilt. "Is she ... is she going to be all right?"

"We don't know yet. They're running more tests tonight." She can tell by the look on Johnny's face that he is very concerned. "She should have come around by now. This bothers you, doesn't it."

"Yes. How can you work here and see all the pain and suffering and not have it bother you?"

"I didn't say it didn't bother me. Sometimes, like this child ... she has her entire life ahead of her. It breaks my heart. We all see so much pain and suffering. But you have to go on and do all you can do for them. It's my job. It's wonderful when they get well and go home to their family."

"What do you know about her family?"

"Not much. I only see her grandmother and her friend come in to see her."

"I'm sorry. I didn't mean to pry."

"No, that's okay. What gets me is, what kind of a person would hit a little girl and not even have the decency to stop."

Johnny is almost sick to his stomach because this hits home, how the drunk driver hit him and killed his family. He jumps up fast. As he leaves, he turns to Miss Porter. "I've got to get back to work. Thanks for the coffee."

Miss Porter is a little puzzled at how fast he wants to leave the room. She stares after him and shrugs her shoulders. She is a little disappointed that he left. "Sure."

The next day at the hospital, Johnny sees two women talking to Dr. Baker. He assumes they are the persons Miss Porter was talking about, but he can't see their faces and he does not want to hang around. He feels too guilty for what he has done. He feels their pain as if it was his own. Not sure what to do, he rushes on down the hall and out of sight.

Dr. Baker gives Granny and Maxie an update. "I'm afraid it's not too good. Gianna has a subdural hematoma."

Granny, very concerned, asks, "What is that?"

"It's a collection of blood on the brain, which causes compression of the brain."

"Do you need to operate?"

"Yes, right away."

"Will she be okay after the operation?"

"There's no guarantee. But she does have a good chance of fully recovering her mental capabilities since she is so young. We're bringing in a team of surgeons from Ashland. There's no one here qualified to do this type of surgery."

"An expensive operation?"

"Very."

Granny looks over at Maxie, who has been sitting very quietly. "Maxie, will you take me over to my bank tomorrow to draw out my savings?"

"No need. It's all been taken care of."

Granny can't believe what the doctor just said. "What? I don't understand, doctor. By who?"

"All I know is that 150 thousand was delivered to the hospital for her care."

"There must be some mistake."

"No mistake. It came from an anonymous donor."

"But from who? We have no other family."

"All we can think of is that it may have been from the person who hit her." Granny looks curiously at Maxie, then at the doctor. "The important thing now is to get her into surgery. Since it's Monday, we can schedule her for Wednesday afternoon. Dr. Gibb needs a couple of days to clear his schedule."

"Wednesday afternoon then?" Granny's voice quivers.

"In her case the sooner the better. You need to come to the office to sign some consent forms."

"Of course, doctor. I will be right there."

After signing the consent forms, Granny goes back to see Gianna one more time and gives her a good night kiss. Then she and Maxie head home. Granny is very quiet in the car. Maxie breaks the silence. "Hey, what is on your mind, Miss Wallace?"

"Well I was just thinking, that ring that Johnny always wore had some very special powers. Magic powers, he said. He didn't know who the old man was who walked up to him that day and helped him out of the dirt. He put the ring on Johnny's finger and he walked home without his crutches, and he walked fine ever since that day. The ring was in Priscilla's hand when she died, but not before giving life to little Gianna. God does work in mysterious ways."

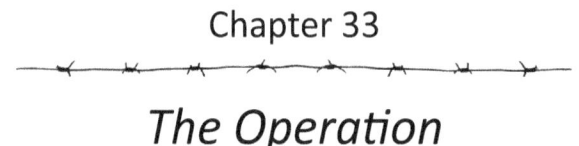

Chapter 33

The Operation

The medical team quickly enters the room. Gianna is lying on the operating table. Other doctors and nurses are around her. The medical team is getting ready for the surgery and they look gravely concerned.

Granny and Maxie are in the waiting room; Granny keeps looking at her watch and pacing the floor. Maxie walks over to her and tries to calm her.

Johnny knows the surgery is going on. Sitting at one of the tables in the cafeteria, he checks the clock on the wall every few minutes. He looks up at the clock again, takes a drink from his cup, notices the sign that says No Smoking but lights a cigarette anyway. He takes a few drags, and then decides to put it out.

Granny and Maxie are still sitting in the waiting room; it's way past midnight and frighteningly silent. Dr. Gibb walks in and goes over to Granny. "Everything went well, now it's a waiting game. Go home and get some rest and come back in the morning. Nothing more we can do."

Chapter 34

The Next Day

*G*ranny and Maxie arrive at the hospital at the break of dawn. Granny goes in to see Gianna. She has monitors hooked up to her; white bandages cover her tiny head. Granny stands by the bed looking down at her, thinking how much she loves this child. She isn't aware that Dr. Gibb has entered the room. He walks over and touches her arm. Granny jumps. "Sorry, I didn't mean to startle you."

"It's okay. How is she doing?"

"She's doing as well as can be expected. We feel the surgery was a success. Now we just have to wait and see, but I'm sure she'll be okay in a week or two."

Granny gives the doctor a hug, as tears roll down her face. "Thank you."

Gianna lies in a coma. Granny sits by her bedside, watching every breath she takes. She takes Gianna's hand in hers. She looks at the small hand, holding it gently and kissing it as more tears roll down her face.

Johnny is busy emptying trash and tidying up the room next to Gianna's. When he exits the room, his eyes focus on room 413. He wants to go in, but he is not sure that he should. He hesitates for a moment. He can't stand it any longer so he opens the door very quietly. He freezes when he sees Gianna's little body lying in the bed. Granny, sitting with her back to the door, doesn't realize that anyone is in the room. Johnny looks at the back of the chair, looks at Gianna, and quietly closes the door.

Chapter 35

Waiting

*G*ranny, again sitting at Gianna's bedside, dozes off. Nurse Porter enters the room; she touches Granny's shoulder, making her jump.

"Oh, I am so sorry, Miss Wallace. Why don't you take a little break?"

"No, I can't."

The nurse sees how tired she looks. "I won't leave her side. I promise."

Granny nods okay and exits the room.

Johnny is rolling his cleaning cart down the hall. He stops at another room. Granny walks down the hall, right beside Johnny. She doesn't notice him, nor does he see her. Johnny enters a room and Granny walks on down the hall.

Chapter 36

Maxie

*M*axie is on the front porch, sitting in her rocking chair. The floor creaks with every rock she takes. She is wearing an apron and has a towel on her lap. The towel is filled with green beans. She picks up one at a time, breaks off the tip, snaps them into pieces, and drops them into a pan sitting beside her. She stops what she is doing as she hears the sound of a car coming down the dirt road, making dust fly. A glimmer of hope crosses her face. As the car gets closer, she sees that it's the mailman. He slows down, but only to wave at her. Maxie goes back to snapping beans. She looks up again when she hears another vehicle approaching. Curious as to who could be coming down the lane and causing more dust, she gets up from her rocking chair, holding the towel in her apron. She walks over to the edge of the porch for a closer look. As the car gets closer, she sees it's a Cadillac convertible with a black man behind the wheel. She lets the beans fall to the floor. She can't believe it. It's Frank! The car pulls up in front of the house and stops. Frank exits the car and, smiling up at Maxie, walks around to the passenger side of the car. "Well, girl, what kind of welcome home is this?"

Maxie is speechless. She unties her apron, raises it over her head, and throws it down on the porch. She runs down the steps and out the gate to Frank's open arms. They can't stop hugging and kissing each other. "Frank, I ..."

Frank looks into her eyes. "Shhh. I'm home." He reaches into the backseat of the car and grabs his suitcase. He puts his arm around Maxie and they walk into the house.

Chapter 37

Thanksgiving

*I*t's a sad time and Granny tries to keep herself busy around her house. She does chores. Feeds Harry and Thelma. Wipes off the 1936 Ford coupe. Rakes leaves. Picks flowers from her garden to take to Gianna.

Granny goes to the doctor's office to speak to Dr. Gibb. "Is there anything I can do?"

"We just don't understand it. She should have recovered months ago. All her vital signs are good. One of the nurses thought she muttered a word today."

"What did she say?"

"Daddy."

"Daddy?"

Dr. Gibb tries to explain. "This could be coming through her subconscious mind. There's no way you could contact her father, is there?"

"No. I wish I could."

"Do you have anything that was her father's that had a big impact on her?"

"Yes. Yes, there is. I will go home right now and get it."

Later that night, way past midnight, Johnny walks down the hall and into Gianna's room. She is lying still in the bed; there is no movement. He walks to the foot of her bed and looks at her for a moment. He's paralyzed by what he sees. He stares at the ring on a chain around Gianna's neck. He walks to the front of the bed. He hesitates, and then very slowly picks up the ring. He hesitates again, and almost puts it back down. Then carefully he puts the ring on his finger. His hand shakes; the ring fits like a glove. He takes the ring off his finger and places it gently back on Gianna's chest. He turns to leave the room. At the moment he reaches the door, the ring glows a bright green. Johnny exits the room, never looking back or seeing the glow. He looks down the long hall, hoping that no one saw him go into the room. All he sees is an old man in a long robe going around the corner. Johnny hurries after him. When he reaches the corner and looks around, he sees no one.

Chapter 38

A Happy Day

Gianna's room is filled with people – doctors, nurses, Granny, Maxie, and Frank. She is awake and sitting up in bed, smiling and enjoying all the attention. The room is very noisy with everyone talking all at once. Dr. Gibb, at Gianna's bedside, says, "Well, young lady, you had quite a nap."

"Yes, I know. But I feel real rested now."

"I bet you do. But you be a good girl and take it easy, and I am sure you will be home for Christmas."

"Christmas? What happened to the Fourth of July?"

Everyone in the room laughs. Granny tells her, "You had a long nap."

"I guess so. What happened to the puppy?"

"You remember?"

"And Bobbie Jo."

Granny knows that she is back to normal and is going to be okay. Gianna reaches up and gives Granny a long hug.

"I missed you."

Tears roll down Granny's face. "And I missed you, child."

Gianna looks around the room and at Maxie. "And old Frank came home."

Everyone in the room laughs. Maxie smiles. "That he did, and thanks to you."

Chapter 39

Johnny Meets Gianna

*J*ohnny, on the night shift, comes into Gianna's room. She is sleeping. As he cleans the room, Gianna wakes up. She looks at Johnny, who is unaware that she is awake. "Hi."

Johnny jumps and stares at her, not believing what he is seeing. "Hi. You're awake."

"Yes. My name is Gianna. What's yours?"

"Mr. ... Brown."

"Nice to meet you, Mr. Brown."

Johnny studies her for a moment. "Likewise."

"So what do you do here? Are you sick?"

"No. I just clean up things, like when you spill milk all over the floor."

As Johnny mops the floor, Gianna says, "I am sorry. Are you mad at me?"

"Of course not. If you didn't spill things, I wouldn't have a job." He finishes cleaning the room. "Well, good night."

"Good night, Mr. Brown."

Chapter 40

Welfare Officer Returns

*I*t's early in the morning at the hospital; Kevin Hughes and Alice Jones walk down the hall. "I don't know if we should see the child without her grandma being here," Kevin says.

That annoys Alice. "Hogwash. This is the best way to get to the truth."

"Well, so far everything Miss Wallace said checks out."

Alice gives him a stern look. "Just shut up and come on."

They reach room 413. Alice looks around and marches into the room; Kevin follows. Gianna is sitting up in bed, coloring. "Hi."

Trying her best to be sweet, Alice replies, "Hi. How are you feeling today?"

"I'm feeling fine. Are you a doctor?"

Kevin, standing at the foot of the bed, says nothing, but he is uncomfortable and sighs loudly. Alice gives him a dirty look. "No, we're from social services. We just came to see if everyone is treating you okay."

"Oh yes. I like all the nurses and the doctor."

"Well, that's good. I want to ask some questions about your home. Does your granny take naps in the daytime?"

"Well, sometimes."

Alice continues to pry. "Then who watches you?"

"Oh, usually Harry does."

"And who is Harry? Your grandpa?"

"Heavens no. Harry is a goat."

Kevin starts to laugh; Alice gives him yet another dirty look. "Well, isn't your granny afraid you'll get hurt all by yourself?"

"Shucks no. There is no one else out there except Maxie and Frank and all my animals and friends. And like Granny says, the animals are better friends than most people. They don't try and hurt no one."

Kevin clears his throat. Alice looks at him and motions for him to leave. They both exit the room. Kevin laughs. "Don't you want to go out and play with Harry?"

"Oh shut up!" Alice is clearly aggravated.

Kevin looks at Alice. "Just give it up. She's been through a lot. She is normal and seems very happy, and she is being taken care of."

Chapter 41

The Date

*J*ohnny is sitting in the cafeteria, eating dinner. Miss Porter enters and comes over and sits down by him. She is glad to see him, but she keeps this to herself. "Where have you been keeping yourself?"

Johnny smiles at her. "Why, did you miss me?"

She is a little embarrassed, but says, "Not at all."

"Hey, I was only kidding. I traded shifts with another guy for a while."

"But you know about Gianna?"

"Oh yes. She spills something every night so I can come in and clean it up. I made the mistake of telling her I won't have a job if I don't have things to clean up. She's making sure I can retire from here."

Miss Porter laughs. "How cute. We all were praying for her."

"I'm glad she is going to be all right." About that time Johnny's pager goes off. He pulls it off of his belt and looks at it. He smiles at Miss Porter. "Guess who. There seems to be a cleanup in room 413. Our little princess is calling." He gets up to leave.

"Johnny?"

He turns toward her. "Yes?"

"Oh nothing. Forget it."

He walks back to where she is sitting; they obviously like each other. "What?"

"I was just wondering … would you like to come over for supper some night?"

"Why, Miss Porter, I'd love too."

She smiles at him. "Please call me Ambra."

Johnny starts to walk out but decides to turn around and yell across the room, so all the people in the cafeteria can hear him. "When?"

The cafeteria becomes quiet as everyone waits for her response. Miss Porter is now quite embarrassed. "Tomorrow night." All the people in the cafeteria clap their hands.

"Eight o'clock okay?"

Miss Porter shakes her head yes. "Eight o'clock."

Johnny has a huge grin on his face as he leaves the room.

Chapter 42

Johnny and Gianna Talk

Johnny is down on his hands and knees cleaning up some water. Gianna is propped up in bed, watching his every move. He finishes his task and looks at Gianna. "Is there anything else I can do for you?"

"Could you stay and talk?"

Johnny is taken by this request. "For a while. So how are you feeling today?"

"I feel fine. I just have one problem."

"What's that?"

"Those two people from social services came to see me, but I heard Granny say they're from welfare."

"What did they want?"

"They asked me some questions."

"Like what."

"Like did my daddy come home yet. And is Harry the only one who watches me when I'm playing."

"Harry?"

"He's my goat."

"Oh, I see. And did you father come home?"

Gianna looks at Johnny straight in the eyes. "No.

But Granny says he'll come home someday, and that he loves me, but he just doesn't know it yet."

Johnny is a little confused. "Well, if that's what your granny says, then she must know what she's talking about."

"I hope so. He's been gone a long time."

Johnny sits on the edge of the bed. "Well, listen. Don't you worry that pretty little head about anything. The most important thing right now is for you to get well. I understand you'll go home before Christmas."

"Mr. Brown, I do have one important wish for Christmas."

"I bet you want a pony or something."

She looks at Johnny very seriously. "I want you to come to my house Christmas Eve and have Christmas with me."

Johnny turns his head away. This really shocks him. After all, he is the one who put her in the hospital. He doesn't want Gianna to see his tears, so he fights them back as he remembers Christmases past.

"Do you not like Christmas, Mr. Brown?"

"Yes, I like Christmas. But I don't think I ..."

"It's my only wish for Christmas. You could meet Harry and Thelma and Maxie, old Frank and Granny. We'll have the best Christmas ever, I promise. Oh please say yes, Mr. Brown. We'll have a big supper and we can sing Christmas carols, you can watch me open my presents and I ..."

"Okay. I'll be there."

Gianna is so excited; she reaches up and gives him a big hug. As he gets ready to leave the room, she looks at him very seriously. "You won't forget, will you?"

He looks back at her. "I'll be there."

"Good. I had better get some sleep now. Good night, Mr. Brown."

"Good night." Before he barely gets the words out of his mouth, she is asleep. He looks at her for a few minutes, then picks up his cleaning bucket and leaves the room.

Chapter 43

Christmas Eve

*T*he little shack is completely decorated with Christmas lights. The lights are all colors, and some of them blink on and off. A beautiful green decorated Christmas tree stands in the front window. The full moon shines brightly high in the sky; the ground is covered with snow. The place is a winter wonderland.

It's early evening and Granny is preparing supper. She opens the oven door and takes a peek at the turkey. Gianna is busy setting the table. A red poinsettia sits in the middle of the table. Red placemats and napkins line the outside of the table. Christmas music plays softly from the record player on a stand.

Johnny travels down the snow-covered road; it's snowing hard and it's very difficult to see out the window of his old truck. He notices that the truck is riding bumpy and the steering wheel is vibrating. He pulls over to the side of the road, stops and exits the truck. He walks around to the back of the truck and shines his flashlight on his back tire.

Meanwhile, back at Granny and Gianna's house,

Granny is at the fireplace, poking the fire with a poker. Gianna is twirling around in her new red velvet dress. Granny looks at her and smiles. "So, you like that new dress, huh?"

Gianna walks over and gives Granny a big hug. "Yes. It's my favorite dress now and my favorite color, red. It's store boughten."

"Store bought."

There's a knock at the front door. It opens and Maxie and Frank walk in. "It's just us, folks. Merry Christmas, Gianna and Granny." At the same time, they both say Merry Christmas to Maxie and Frank.

Maxie carries in a dish. Gianna, eager to see what it is, asks, "What did you make, Maxie?"

"Black-eyed peas."

"Yuk. Black-eyed peas?"

Granny gives Gianna the eye. "Mind your manners." Maxie and Frank can't help but laugh.

Gianna notices that Frank is carrying a plate also. She looks at him as if to ask what it is.

Frank reads her mind. "It's all your favorite cookies and candy."

She takes one. Granny warns her, "Only one. I don't want you to spoil your supper."

"I won't, I promise. I'm hungry."

Maxie motions for Gianna to come over to where she is sitting by the fire. "Let me look at you, child. You sure do look pretty." Frank agrees.

Gianna answers quickly, sure of herself. "I know."

Granny scolds her again. "Gianna."

"Well, I do look pretty."

"I know, but you don't have to agree."

"You mean, if Maxie thinks I'm pretty and Frank thinks I'm pretty and you think I'm pretty and I think I'm pretty … I'm not pretty?"

They all try not to laugh. Frank and Maxie look at Granny to see what she is going to say. "Well, I guess you have a point. Yes, you are very pretty. I better go look at the turkey."

"Thank you all." Gianna swings around the room in her new store-boughten dress.

Back out on the snow-covered road, Johnny is trying very hard to get the lug nuts off the tire with the lug wrench, but to no avail. He strains and struggles, but they won't turn. He gets up and goes around the truck to the driver's side. He opens the door and looks inside to see if there is anything else he can use. He finds a hammer and takes it around the side of the truck. To his amazement all the lug nuts are laying on the ground in the snow. He has an eerie feeling and looks up and down the road to see if anybody is there. He sees no one. He removes the flat tire and lays it down on the ground. Then he stares at the snow-covered ground. He sees two bare footprints in the snow. As he looks at them, they disappear before his eyes.

Chapter 44

The Best Christmas Ever

Supper is cooking. The fire crackles. The Christmas tree in front of the window shines brightly with all colors of bulbs covering the tree. They are listening to Christmas music. On the end table is a clock that Gianna keeps watching. Also on the table is the wooden lion with Johnny's ring around its neck.

Maxie looks at Gianna. "So when is this special friend of yours coming?"

"Any time. Maybe he got lost."

"I'm sure he'll be here real soon. Why don't you let Frank read you a Christmas story. I will go help Miss Wallace with supper."

Maxie walks into the kitchen as Granny is taking the turkey out of her wood-burning stove. Maxie inhales deeply. "Mmm mmm. Never thought that ugly turkey could smell so good."

Granny sets the turkey on the table. "Gianna wanted everything perfect tonight for her guest."

"So who is this special friend she's got coming, Miss Wallace?"

"I don't know. She's been so secretive. One of the kids she met at the hospital, I guess."

Gianna and Frank are looking at a Christmas book. Every few minutes she looks at the clock. Granny hollers from the kitchen. "Supper will be ready in ten minutes, so get your hands washed."

Gianna yells back. "Okay, and I just know he is on his way." She gets up from the couch and walks over to the end table. She picks up the ring and holds it for a few moments. She closes her eyes. Her lips move like she is saying a prayer or making a silent wish.

Johnny pulls up outside. He stares at the beautiful decorations and, almost in a trance, thinks of his house all decorated years ago. He shuts off the engine and exits his truck. He walks toward the front door; he hesitates a moment, and he hears the people inside singing 'Santa Claus is coming to town.' He is carrying two small gifts.

Gianna's eyes light up when she hears a knock on the door. She is so happy that her special friend has finally arrived. All the food is on the table. Granny takes off her apron and goes to the door. She opens it and looks down, expecting to see a kid, but instead she looks up and sees her son standing there. She stares at him. There is dead silence in the room. Then she screams. "Johnny!"

Johnny is stunned to see his mother. "I thought you were dead!"

Granny throws her arms around him. "Johnny, my son. You came home."

Gianna stands there; she can't move. Johnny looks down at her. She looks up at him with a smile on her face. "Daddy?" Granny lets go of Johnny. He bends down and reaches out his arms to Gianna. "My daddy came home!"

Maxie and Frank are overjoyed at the reunion. The ring on the table glows brightly again. They all look out the big picture window. It's snowing lightly. The full moon shining on the snow is brighter than ever. An old man is walking away from the house, his robe slightly moving in the wind. He walks toward the lane. This time he leaves no footprints in the snow.

- The End -

Gianna's Family

Mamie Jean Calvert is an extremely talented screenwriter who won Writer of the Year at the AOF Film Festival for her script *Sunshine*. She also won best screenplay for *Murder by Design*. She has been involved in the entertainment industry for over 25 years.

During her long career, Mamie Jean produced and directed more than 200 cable television shows and more than a dozen shorts for Channel 52 in Los Angeles. She wrote shows for the Los Angeles Sheriff's Department to help with their D.A.R.E. program. She also produced and directed a dozen 10-minute shorts for Beverly Hills High School for one semester. She has won 25 awards in various categories.

Mamie Jean wrote and produced the feature film *In the Eyes of a Killer/Blindsided*, directed by and starring Louis Mandylor of *My Big Fat Greek Wedding* and many others. *In the Eyes of a Killer/Blindsided* also stars Costas Mandylor (*Saw* movies), James Marshall (*Twin Peaks, A Few Good Men*), Gwendolyn Edwards (*The Last Confederate*), and Petri Hawkins-Byrd (*Judge Judy*). The movie was released by Monarch Films and has won twelve film awards.

Mamie Jean Calvert owns Ambra Productions LLC. Her film credits may be viewed at www.imdb.com.

www.ingramcontent.com/pod-product-compliance
Lightning Source LLC
Chambersburg PA
CBHW071405170626
46811CB00003B/1260